The Christmas Roommate

A SPENCER BROTHERS CHRISTMAS SHORT STORY

ANA ASHLEY

The Christmas Roommate- A Spencer Brothers Christmas Short Story
© 2023 by Ana Ashley
First Edition: Nov 2023

ALL RIGHTS RESERVED
No part of this publication may be reproduced, distributed, or transmitted in any form or by any means, including photocopy, recording, or other electronic or mechanical methods, without the prior written permission of the author, except in the case of brief quotations embodied in critical reviews and certain noncommercial uses permitted by copyright law.

The Christmas Roommate is a work of fiction. Names, characters, businesses, places events and incidents are either products of the author's imagination or used in a fictitious manner. Any resemblance to actual persons, living or dead, or actual events is purely coincidental.

Cover design: Natasha Snow Designs

Cover Model: Shawn O'Neill

Photography by Golden Czermak / FuriousFotog

Editor: Abbie Nicole

Join Ana's Facebook Group Café RoMMance for exclusive content, and to learn more about the latest books at anawritesmm.com!

Dedication

⸎

To everyone who isn't afraid to feel the feelings.
To everyone who's brave enough to act on them.

Merry Christmas!

Ana

x

Keep an eye on Ren, they said.
Just for tonight, they said.

Next thing you know, I'm babysitting three-hundred succulents and Ren is making himself at home in my space.
Not only do I welcome his company, I crave it. And that little doubt I had about my sexuality? Obliterated in a few short months.

The problem? How to show Ren I want to be more than just his friend.
The plan? Convince him to be my roommate for Christmas and hope he'll stay forever.

The Christmas Roommate is a standalone Christmas short story set in Ana's new world of the Spencer brothers.
Expect lots of pining from two guys who secretly love each other, an adorable puppy, and the biggest collection of succulents in the history of romance.

Frederick

I have an extra ticket for The Nutcracker tonight. Want to join me?

Who bailed on you?

Lex. He's stuck at work.

You mean he found a genuine reason to avoid the torture?

The Nutcracker isn't torture. It's enchanting and some of the best music ever composed.

I'll take your word for it, but I can't join you. Ren's coming over.

. . .

I pocketed my phone as I saw the speech bubbles appear and disappear a few times. Besides, my fingers were freezing from using the phone while I walked the mile from the office to my apartment. It wasn't far enough to take a cab, but it was far enough to freeze any exposed skin.

"*I need a favor*," Emery, my ex-fake boyfriend and new best friend, had said all those months ago.

A favor.

Friends do favors for each other all the time, right? Besides, it wasn't as if I could say no. By agreeing to pretend to date, Emery and I had managed to keep our match-making mothers at bay. This meant we had covered for each other no matter what.

I wasn't even gay, but a white lie I'd told as a teenager stuck to me like a piece of toilet paper under your shoe when you come out of a public restroom.

Despite my plans to spend that evening watching *The Antiques Roadshow*—the British version, of course—I'd been summoned to a diner an hour outside town.

Emery never warned me how that one night would change me forever. He couldn't have known. He was too busy falling in love with the guy he was supposed to be with for real.

I began removing all the extra layers of clothing as soon as I stepped inside the elevator to go up to my apartment.

After spending most of my twenties in London, I was used to variable weather, especially in winter. It could rain one day and snow the next, but there'd never been snow at Christmas.

I'd missed it then, but now? I welcomed the cozy warmth in my apartment.

It cost me a fortune to keep the place heated when the temperatures outside were at a constant freezing twenty degrees, but I couldn't do anything about that.

Once inside, I hung up my coat and put my bag in the closet, returning to my phone after I turned the coffee pot on. Yes, it was warm inside the apartment, but my bones still felt cold from the December temperatures.

EMERY

Have you told him yet?

FREDERICK

No.

EMERY

When are you going to do it?

FREDERICK

Never?

I could just imagine Ren's face as I broke the news.

You know how I pretended to be gay on a date with Emery and came out as straight because you were hitting on me and being totally obnoxious? Well, it turns out I've changed my mind about you, and I'm not as straight as I thought.

Then we'd laugh it off as Ren would say he was right all along, but we couldn't be together because not only did I have zero experience with guys, but I was totally not his type.

EMERY

Why?

FREDERICK

I'm not his type.

EMERY

Gorgeous, successful, and super nice? I can see how you wouldn't be anyone's type.

I laughed at his next message, which was full of eye-roll emoji.

Emery's relationship was a true love story. He'd fallen in love with Lex and even gotten engaged. But after a car accident left Emery with no memory of the last few years, he'd practically disappeared under the influence of his parents.

Lex had thought Emery had ghosted him, and Emery hadn't known Lex existed until they met by chance and fell in love again.

FREDERICK

Not everyone can have a fairytale love story.

EMERY

But it's Christmas. If you don't take a chance at Christmas, when will you?

FREDERICK

I regret the day I confided in you.

EMERY

Oh, come on, we were practically almost married. If you don't confide in me, who will you confide in?

FREDERICK

In the 300 succulents that live with me. They understand me better.

EMERY

Fine. Be a lonely grump instead of having hot sex with Ren. I'll call one of my brothers instead for The Nutcracker.

I wanted to make a joke about nutcrackers, but I filled a cup with coffee and took it to the window overlooking the park instead. I'd been lucky to find this apartment when I moved back to the States. My parents had wanted me to stay closer to home, but after getting an offer from Emery's dad to run his company before he retired, I knew I needed to be in the city.

Having park views was necessary for someone who'd

grown up in the countryside. Even in Europe, I'd taken every chance I could to escape the city.

The space wasn't too bad either, which was lucky because when I moved in, I never thought I'd be babysitting Ren's collection of succulents.

A favor.

That was all it had been. Making sure Ren didn't get in trouble that night after he'd found out his boyfriend had not only cheated on him repeatedly while they were together, he'd also gotten the poor girl pregnant.

I'd followed Ren as he'd convinced me to break into the guy's place to *steal* his succulent collection. I'd been annoyed enough with the guy for cheating on Ren that I'd done it, but I had severely underestimated the size of the collection.

I looked at the clock on the wall.

"Don't you worry your little plump leaves. Your daddy will be here any time now," I said to the plants. Not surprisingly, just as their owner had grown on me in the most unexpected way, so had they.

I'd followed the strict instruction not to water them, but I often found myself talking to them. If that wasn't a sign I needed to get out more, I didn't know what was.

The sound of a key made my heart skip several beats.

I tried to remind myself that he was only here to see his babies and would sleep over only because he had an early start at the flower market, where he worked on Saturdays.

After fifteen years of thinking I was straight, Ren had made me question my sexual orientation from the moment we met.

"Fuck me. It's so cold out that my jingleberries are all shriveled."

I took a calming breath and turned around, sipping my coffee for something to do. "That sounds like an unfortunate thing."

He shrugged. "Doesn't matter how shriveled my jingleberries are when my chances of a jinglejob this year are slim to none."

"A what?"

He set his large duffel bag on the floor and placed his hands on his hips. "A Christmas blowjob."

I choked on my last sip of coffee. I couldn't have images of Ren giving or receiving blowjobs for Christmas in my head.

Not when I'd promised Emery I'd tell Ren about my feelings for him before Christmas. I'd crossed my fingers behind my back, so I wasn't sure it counted, but still.

Ren

"I s it okay if I do some laundry here? My parents' machine is broken again," I asked, avoiding eye contact.

"Sure."

I grabbed the heavy duffel bag and took it to Frederick's pornographic laundry room. Brand new appliances, white walls, organized cupboards with towels neatly folded? It was impossible not to get a laundry boner just by walking in.

Besides, it smelled like Frederick in there. It was the only place I allowed myself to breathe in, smell him, and dream that maybe in another world, he wasn't straight and was into hyperactive twinks who loved wearing shorts and crop tops, even in freezing temperatures.

I pulled all my clothes out of the bag and put them in the machine. Another advantage of using his laundry room was that I would smell like him all week.

Yeah, I was a masochist.

"Hey," Frederick said from the door, making me jump. "Italian, Chinese, or Indian?"

"Hmm, let me think...based on my current plans for sexual activities—i.e., zero—I'd say Indian. If a boy can't get pleasure from one hole, he may as well get it in the other."

Frederick groaned a reply I didn't catch and left me.

I didn't mean to torment Frederick with my jokes or innuendos, but every time he coughed, blushed, or groaned, it was a reminder he was straight and off-limits. I needed that reminder.

I just wished I didn't like far too much that he cuddled with me on the couch, picked my favorite TV show, and gave me the bigger food portion. It gave me ideas I had no business having.

I opened the lid on his laundry basket, and just like I expected, his whites and colors were all mixed up. Yeah, he was still straight.

While we waited for the food, I took a quick shower. Since I came over most Fridays to see my succulents and hang out with Frederick, I already had something to wear in the spare room.

In just a few months, the room had become my sanctuary. A bunch of my succulents were on a desk by the window. The bed was made with a comforter Frederick had given me as a birthday present—turquoise with a mermaid holding a pineapple.

Every time I walked in, I felt at home and hated it simultaneously. I shouldn't get used to these comforts. It only made the rest of my week so much harder in comparison.

If Frederick knew what I was hiding, he'd probably make me move in for good. I couldn't handle that. Watching him as he went out on dates, or worse, if he brought them to stay the night. Ew, no. Listening to straight sex would be the ultimate torture.

"Dinner's here," he shouted from the kitchen.

I walked out, wearing my pajama shorts with the unicorns and a cropped shirt with rainbows. Even though I'd had an exhausting day, wearing clothes I liked always cheered me up.

Frederick had already plated our dinner, so I joined him at the table. My plate had the biggest portion.

Gah, he had no right to be this kind and straight.

"How was your day?" he asked.

"It was good. Tiring."

"What job did you do today? No. Let me guess."

I doubted he would get it right, but I entertained him. We played this game every week.

Was he even aware that most of the jobs I admitted to doing wouldn't even pay enough for a week's rent?

"You walked dogs today."

I shook my head and filled my fork with delicious butter chicken and rice.

"Warehouse porter."

"Nope."

He tapped his chin with his finger.

"If you don't hurry up, I'll finish my food and then eat yours."

His smile reached into my belly and twisted it into knots, dammit. Why did he have to have dimples on top of everything else? The muscles, the kindness, the sense of humor? I should hate him.

"You came in smiling, so maybe you got a job in a flower store."

I wish. "Bingo!"

"I knew it. Will you work there again?"

I nodded, keeping my mouth busy with food. Under no circumstances would I ever admit that I'd scored a gig cleaning naked for people. What could I say? There were weird people out there, and I needed their money. So if they got their kicks from seeing me mop their floors and dust their shelves while naked, I'd oblige, as long as they kept their hands to themselves, which they had...so far.

"How close are you now?" he asked.

"Getting there." That was always my answer. My life-long dream was to own a flower store, but that had been shattered when my trashy ex cheated on me, putting an end to my dream of buying his parents' flower store with him.

After the tragic—or lucky, depending on how you looked at it—night when Frederick helped me rescue my succulents and teach Chad a lesson, I'd had to change my plan.

I couldn't afford to move to the city, but the city jobs paid more. All I needed was to work all the jobs available to someone low-skilled like me and save as much as possible so the bank would give me a business loan to open my very own flower store.

Frederick thought I was commuting to and from my parents' place outside the city, but the sad reality was that I was living in my car.

Occasionally, when I didn't spend at least one night here, I'd pay for a cheap motel with laundry facilities, but those cut into my savings target, so I kept them to a minimum. But it was becoming harder and harder.

Of all winters, this one decided it would be the winterest winter that has ever wintered.

"How's your work? Do anything important this week?" I asked, keen on diverting the conversation away from me.

"I did lots of things, but their importance will depend on who you ask."

"I still can't believe you're working for Emery's dad." My eyes tracked his Adam's apple as he drank a sip of water.

"I know. I wouldn't have accepted the job if it wasn't for Emery. I hate what his parents did to him by lying when he had the accident that caused the amnesia."

"But you like the job, right?"

"Yeah, I do. Without this opportunity, it would have taken me a long time to get to where I am now. I'm not saving the world, but I love figuring out investment opportunities, returns, and especially turning around a non-profitable business."

I spent the rest of dinner listening to Frederick talk about his work. He was so incredibly smart. Much smarter than I'd ever be. He would never let himself get taken for a ride like I had with my ex.

After dinner, I insisted on doing the dishes while he picked something for us to watch on TV.

"*The Antiques Roadshow* again?" I asked.

"You know you love it."

"I'm partial to the accent. I'll give you that. But not when you do it. Your British accent is terrible."

He feigned shock. "How could you say that?" he asked in the worst accent, and I raised a brow.

I brought us each a cup of tea and placed them on the coffee table. Frederick pulled me by the waist until I fell on the couch, as close to him as I could be with clothes on.

It was pure torture.

Did I need to tell him that straight men were my kryptonite? That somehow, even though I knew they'd never be mine, I couldn't stop myself from being attracted?

I was cursed. That's what it was. When I was a baby, my parents threw a party to welcome their firstborn into the world, and someone cursed me to feel attraction only to those who will never reciprocate.

"That's a big sigh you let out," Frederick said. "Wanna talk about it?"

"I'm just wondering how people don't check their attics for decades and then find these priceless treasures. If we went through my parents' attic, all we'd find is my cheerleading trophies, old clothes, and maybe my dad's old fishing gear."

Frederick tightened his hold on me and then tickled my sides. "You never told me you were a cheerleader."

"There's plenty of things I haven't told you about me."

"Like what?"

Like I think I'm in love with you, which goes beyond any attraction I've ever felt for another man, and it's scary, sad, and frustrating. That's what I wanted to say, but what came out was, "I'll tell you my secrets if you tell me yours."

He laughed. "You wouldn't believe my secrets."

I wanted to argue and make him talk, even though I did not intend to reveal my secrets. I'd have to make one up. But he pointed at the TV where the presenter had just gone wide-eyed over a ceramic vase.

I must have fallen asleep at some point because when I opened my eyes, there was no sound from the TV and my head was on Frederick's chest.

I looked up to see he was looking back at me and smiling.

"What? Did I drool?" I sat up, reaching up to my mouth with my hand. Thankfully, my skin was dry. How embarrassing would it have been to drool on the sexiest men you'd ever met?

Mortifying.

"You didn't drool."

"Um, okay then, maybe I should get to bed. I'll be out before six tomorrow."

Frederick narrowed his eyes. "You look tired," he said.

"I've been busy. Don't worry. I'm sure I'll have some time off for Christmas."

"You're...sure?"

I shrugged. What could I say? If my naked cleaning client wanted to pay me to clear his Christmas party leftovers, I'd do it. A single day doing that work paid as much as a whole week walking dogs or packing groceries.

"Oh," I said, halfway to the bedroom, "next Sunday is my sister's Christmas school play. Do you want to come?"

"I'd love to. Should I bring her a gift?"

Be still my beating heart.

"Only if you want to. She'll be happy enough with her fans there, and you know how much she loves you."

His smile made my stomach flutter a little. He even adored my sister. Could he be any more perfect? Where was the obnoxious jackass with the fake British accent I'd first met?

"Will you come back to the city with me after the show? I'd like to decorate a Christmas tree," Frederick asked.

"You...want me to decorate a Christmas tree with you?"

He rolled his eyes. "Well, yeah. You know more about coordinating colors and shit. If it's up to me, it'll be a mismatch of colors and decorations."

Ah, of course. "Sure, it'll be fun. I'm going to bed now, okay?"

"Okay."

Maybe I was too exhausted from not sleeping properly and working every day, but I suddenly felt more vulnerable and raw than usual.

"Hey, Frederick?" I called from the bedroom door.

"Yeah?"

"Thank you for letting me use your laundry room."

"Anytime, sweetheart."

I sighed. I was so in love with that man that I should be committed to an institution. Still, only a few more months until I had enough money, and then I'd have my little store with a small studio on the second floor that would be my home. I'd take all my succulents and wouldn't need to see Frederick as often.

I could hold on to that dream, right?

Frederick

One of the many things I loved about Ren was the way he expressed himself through his clothes. He was always bright, cheerful, and full of energy. No matter where he was, he was always himself.

I, on the other hand, had spent so many years building an image that sometimes I wasn't even sure who I was. The suits I wore to work felt comfortable when I was at work. They told people I belonged there. I could be trusted to know what I was doing.

Outside of work? Sometimes, I wished I was a little braver. Not that I'd wear shorts and tiny tops, like Ren, but I wasn't sure which version of dressy-casual or casual-casual was more me.

I had a wardrobe full of clothes I rarely wore.

"I'm ready if you—" Ren stopped speaking, staring at me still in my boxer shorts.

"I don't know what to wear," I confessed.

He huffed and pushed past me into the walk-in closet.

"Honest to god, Frederick Rhys-Myr, if you sold all your clothes, I'd have enough money to buy my dream flower store outright. You certainly have enough."

Two seconds later, he returned with a pair of jeans, a Henley, and a red sweater I'd bought ages ago but had never worn because it was red. I didn't know what passed through my head when I bought it.

"Well?" He crossed his arms, waiting for me to put the clothes on.

It's not that I didn't trust his choices, but I didn't want to look out of place with Ren's family. They were everything mine wasn't: warm, funny, welcoming, down to earth. The last thing I wanted was to look like a wealthy, pompous ass.

I put on the clothes and looked in the mirror. Okay, I'd admit I looked...like nothing special. The clothes fit perfectly, but because I wasn't wearing a dress shirt, I looked ready for a family day out instead of a casual meeting in the city.

"Thank you," I said.

"Anytime. Now, let's go. Winnie will never forgive us if we're late and miss her big song."

On the way out, I grabbed Winnie's gift and followed Ren. He stopped between our cars, sitting side by side in the parking lot.

"Erm, would you mind if we take your car? I have a lot of junk to take to Goodwill, so mine's messy. That conversation we had last week about attics got me thinking, so I cleaned mine out, but I haven't had time to take all the... um...stuff."

"Of course. I don't mind driving."

Ren practically ran to the passenger side of my car, keeping his head down and his hands in his pockets.

"Come on, we'll be late."

"All right, all right," I said, making my way to the car.

As I opened the door, I glanced at Ren's car. It had a few bags in the back seat, but it wasn't untidy. There were a few shirts on hangers, and I noticed a toiletry bag.

It didn't look like the kind of stuff you'd take to Goodwill, but he was fidgeting in his seat, so I didn't ask. If he was anxious about getting to his sister's show on time, I'd make it happen.

Sunday traffic out of town wasn't too bad, and after receiving a message from Ren's mom to meet them at Winnie's school, we changed the route and got there with time to spare.

Ren's mom, wearing a dress with a Christmas tree pattern and little decorations hanging from the hem, ran to him as soon as we parked.

"I'm so glad you're here. Winnie is already inside."

She hugged Ren like she hadn't seen him in a while. His eyes met mine, and I smiled when he rolled his eyes at his mom's over-the-top greeting.

When she let him go, she gave me a tight hug. "So nice to see you too, Frederick. I'm glad you could come."

"The pleasure is all mine, Mrs. Oliver. I wouldn't miss Winnie's show for the world."

She shepherded us inside the makeshift theater the school had set up in the gym. Ren's dad waved at us from where he was holding our seats.

"I don't think I've ever been to a school show," I said to Ren as we sat.

He crossed one leg over the other and wrapped his arms around mine, giving me no choice but to place my hand on his knee. Did he know what he was doing to me? Or was he so sure of my heterosexuality that he didn't think I'd care?

Once, when Ren had what he called a Chadlapse—a relapse following his breakup, in which he got drunk on red wine and ice cream—he'd told me he had a weakness for straight guys.

At the time, I'd still been trying to figure out why my eyes couldn't move away from him, why my heart jilted when he was nearby, and why his proximity caused erections. I didn't think I was one of those "straight" guys he felt attracted to because despite him being very tactile with me and borderline flirty, he never indicated we were more than friends. In fact, he seemed to mention our friendship at any given opportunity.

This was why, despite what I'd promised Emery, I knew I couldn't come out to Ren and tell him about my feelings because I'd ruin the best friendship I'd ever had.

He squeezed my hand, and I swallowed. He may as well have squeezed the lower parts of my body that loved whenever he was this close.

"Look, that's her class. I remember a few of her friends." He pointed to the stage where a group of students had positioned themselves in a circle.

The lights dimmed as a spotlight shone on a corner of the stage. I recognized her straight away. At ten years old, Winnie was the carbon copy of her older brother, with her blonde hair, button nose, and big brown eyes. She wore a red dress with shiny red high heels, and her long hair was tied up in a bun.

I heard a sniffle and looked at Ren, who was fanning his face with his hand. Ren's mom was moving her hand in time to the music as if she were directing her daughter, who raised the microphone to her mouth and began singing.

"Wow. You never said Winnie could sing like that," I whispered.

He nodded fiercely, a few tears running down his cheek.

I'd heard Winnie play the piano many times. She was a true natural musical talent. Ren kept saying she was going to Juilliard as soon as she turned sixteen.

I would never dismiss his feelings or dreams, but even with Winnie's talent, it wasn't cheap to attend Juilliard, and it would likely require one or both of his parents to move to New York with Winnie.

Winnie had a beautiful voice. When the song ended, there was a standing ovation. She blushed and thanked the audience before joining the other students around the circle.

Another piece of music I didn't recognize started playing.

"Oh, they're doing *The Nutcracker*," Ren said. "It's my favorite."

I smiled to myself. I'd have to tell Emery I ended up watching a slightly different version of *The Nutcracker*.

The show lasted a couple of hours, with more students showcasing their singing, dancing, and music-playing talents.

When we met Winnie outside, she was jumping up and down like she'd taken a happy drug or drank five cups of coffee.

"Freddy! You came!" she shouted as she ran toward me, practically jumping into my arms.

"Hey, kiddo. You did amazing today. Congratulations." I hugged her back and set her on the ground. Next to me, Ren laughed.

"How about me? Am I chopped liver?" Ren asked, crossing his arms. "It's all about Freddy, huh?"

I stuck my tongue out to him. Winnie was the only one who'd ever given me a nickname, and while Freddy wasn't the best one, I kinda liked it when it came from her.

"Hi, Laurence. Thank you for coming to the show," she said, rolling her eyes while full-naming her brother. I thought she was joking the first time she said it, but then he'd told me he was named after a laurel wreath that symbolizes victory, triumph, and success.

Considering his parents had tried for years to have a baby before Ren came along, it made sense. Winnie had been a complete surprise to the couple, so she'd been given a name that meant joy and peace.

Winnie said goodbye to her friends and teacher, and then we all went to Ren's parents' place, where his mom had made a cake to celebrate Winnie's Christmas show.

"Mom, when are we going to decorate our Christmas tree?" Winnie asked. "Clara said she's doing it this weekend because her big sister is visiting from college."

"We can do it tomorrow if Dad brings the decorations down from the attic."

Mr. Oliver ate the last bite of his cake and finished his coffee. Ren was still halfway through his but stood when his dad bumped his shoulder.

"Figures," he mumbled as he followed his dad. "You owe me, kiddo. I better have the best Christmas card this year."

Winnie giggled and carried on eating her cake.

I helped Mrs. Oliver clear the plates.

"Frederick, can I ask you a question?"

"Of course."

"Do you think everything's okay with Ren?"

I put a plate in the dishwasher and turned to face her. "What do you mean?"

She looked toward the kitchen door before she said, "He looks tired. I'm afraid he's taken on too many jobs. I know he wants to get his own shop, and god knows he's stubborn enough to make it happen, but I don't want it to be detrimental to his health. He knows he doesn't need to work so hard."

"You know your son. Getting a shop is everything to him. Rent in the city isn't cheap. I'm sure he knows how much he needs to save upfront. He's very smart."

She sighed. "He should use the money. It's there for him. I would try to convince him, but these days, I'm lucky if I see him once every three weeks."

That was a loaded statement, and I needed answers.

"I'm sorry, Mrs. Oliver. I don't want to pry, but what do you mean?"

She picked up the rest of the plates and stacked them in the dishwasher.

"He has all the money his grandfather left him. I know he said it should be used for Winnie when she gets into Juilliard, but we don't even know if she'll get in, and in the meantime, he's killing himself working so hard."

I put a hand on her shoulder. "I'll talk to him."

Except I didn't because when we got back to my place, Ren went into the bathroom to grab a shower, which gave me the opportunity to check on something.

I grabbed his car keys and went outside. The toiletry bag I'd noticed earlier in the backseat of his car was filled with his favorite shampoo, soap, and all the stuff he already had in my bathroom when he stayed over.

I opened one of the bags, and his favorite sweater was right on top. The shirts hanging from the handle were his work shirts from the Italian riverfront restaurant, where he worked three nights a week.

Ren wasn't giving old stuff to Goodwill. He was fucking living in his car.

I locked his car and went straight up to my room, making sure to leave his keys where I'd found them.

I was angry, disappointed, and sad. There were so many feelings going through me that I needed time alone to process them before I did or said something stupid that drove Ren away. At least I knew he'd be safe and warm tonight.

What the fuck are you doing living in a car in the middle of winter, Ren?

Ren

I pulled my coat collar up around my face. I knew I should have booked a room for tonight. It was easily the coldest night so far.

I'd used the car's heater until I had to turn it off to not deplete the battery. It lasted long enough that I thought I'd fall asleep, but I felt restless today, and I wasn't entirely sure it was due to the cold.

As Frederick and I were leaving my parents' place on Sunday, my mom had given me a look I knew as her momma-bear gaze. She knew something was up, and I would be stupid not to see it coming.

"Ugh, just go to sleep, dammit," I shouted in frustration. If I fell asleep at work tomorrow, I'd get in trouble. As it was, Mr. Wilson, the owner of the grocery store where I stocked shelves twice a week, had already given me a warning after I accidentally fell asleep in the storeroom.

In my defense, he'd made me do a super late shift the day before, so I hadn't even driven out of the parking lot to my usual spot. I'd slept right there and had been the first one in.

Either way, I couldn't afford to lose this job. The store, the restaurant, and the flower market on Saturdays were my fixed jobs. Those guaranteed I could eat, sometimes sleep in a real bed, and save some money. The other jobs were less regular, although my naked cleaning client suggested yesterday that I go in twice a week each week and extra when they threw dinner parties.

I'd also discovered that his request for naked cleaning had nothing to do with a weird fetish. Apparently, his previous cleaners had stolen some family heirlooms, and this was the only way they figured they wouldn't get robbed.

He'd even agreed I could start wearing boxer shorts because I'd earned his trust by doing a good job and not once given him reason to think I might steal something.

If only my solid work ethic and being a good person were enough to make my dreams come true.

A knock on the car window made me jump.

"Shit. Shit."

"Sir, can you roll the window down, please?"

I sat up and looked around like I was guilty of stashing drugs or holding a dead body in the car.

The policeman didn't knock again, so maybe I was in luck tonight. The first time I'd been caught sleeping in the car, the officer threatened to take me to the station.

"Hi, um...officer," I mumbled as I rolled down the window.

"Are you aware you are not allowed to sleep in a car out here?"

I straightened my hair using my fingers. "Yes, sir. I wasn't sleeping. Well, I was hoping to sleep, but only to rest my eyes for a moment. You see"—I pointed to the back of the car—"I'm traveling a long way, and I was getting tired. I couldn't find a place to stay, so I figured I'd close my eyes for a couple of hours and then move on."

He gave me a look that told me he didn't believe me, but thankfully, he didn't ask for my ID.

"There's a motel two blocks that way on the right. They have rooms. Put your head on a pillow, and you'll probably avoid an accident on the road."

I nodded. "Yes, sir. Thank you."

He tapped the hood of the car and walked away. I let out a long sigh of relief and started the car. I didn't stop until I was in the parking lot of a shopping mall with a twenty-four-hour diner next door, so some cars were always parked there.

I'd avoided it in the past because it could get too noisy, but tonight, I'd take the noise instead of jail.

Once I'd layered with two extra sweaters and pairs of gloves and covered my head with a scarf, I fell asleep. By the time my alarm went off in the morning, I was ready to drive straight to Frederick's place and ask if I could crawl into his spare bed and stay there forever.

And if he could cuddle me, that would be an extra bonus.

I straightened myself and used the bottle of water I carried in the car to brush my teeth. Then I packed a protein bar and made myself a coffee with the travel kettle, putting it in a to-go cup.

Mr. Wilson was waiting for me with a list of chores a mile long. I usually didn't mind because extra time meant extra money, but I was so tired that I just wanted to go away.

"Ren, I need you to do a home delivery for me," Mr. Wilson said, coming into the produce aisle where I was stacking the vegetables in color order. It was a suggestion I'd made weeks ago, and sales had gone up, so he'd let me keep it up.

"Sure thing."

It felt good going outside. The cold air was so refreshing that once I checked how far the delivery was, I decided to walk there instead of driving.

It was very nice of Mr. Wilson to arrange home delivery for some of the older customers who didn't want to come out when it was this cold and with the threat of a snowstorm.

The delivery didn't take me longer than thirty minutes, but I felt so energized after the walk that I knew I could easily handle the rest of the day at the store. I didn't have any other jobs, so I would check into the motel for the night and catch up on sleep.

When I got back to the store, Mr. Wilson looked angry.

"Did anything happen while I was gone?" I asked.

"Yes. I lost twenty bucks because you priced the laundry detergent at seven bucks instead of twenty-seven."

Shit.

"I'm so sorry, Mr. Wilson. I don't know how that

happened. I'll pay you the money you lost and fix the prices now."

His shoulders sagged. "Look, Ren, I like you, and the customers like you, but this kind of stuff can't keep happening. It's not just about the money. You need to be focused and awake. I'll let this one slide because I did give you a long list of stuff today, but I need you to pay attention to the rest of it and then go home and get some rest when you finish."

"Yes, sir. Thank you." My first job was to check the laundry detergent. I found three bottles with the wrong price, and they weren't ones I'd done because they were dusty. I was annoyed that I'd taken the blame for something likely done by the kid who worked in the store during the weekends.

I checked my account and worked on my savings plan during my lunch break. I couldn't continue sleeping in my car like a homeless person when I could rent a room somewhere. Sure, it wouldn't be anything big, but at least it wasn't the car.

I'd save less throughout the cold-weather months, but if I stopped making mistakes at work or doubting myself so much that I took the fall for someone else's mistakes, then it was worth it.

With that resolve, I dug into the reduced sandwich I'd bought from the deli section. Mr. Wilson let us buy food that was going out of date for a discount, so I often did extra shopping after my shift. Most things held out pretty well after the expiration date.

I was about to put my phone back in the locker when it dinged with a message from Frederick.

FREDERICK

Hey, I need a favor. I'm going away for a few days on business. I promised Emery I'd look after their puppy while they're away for a few days. I feel super bad, but I can't cancel this trip. Would you house-sit for me and make sure the puppy is fed?

REN

Of course I will. I didn't know they got a puppy. How cute. What's his name?

FREDERICK

He doesn't have a name yet, so you can call him whatever you want. I'm leaving straight from work. Can you stay here tonight?

I rested my head against the hard metal of the locker. I wasn't sure I believed in Santa or Christmas miracles, but I was pretty sure this was it.

REN

I don't know. If you let me raid your fridge, I may be convinced.

FREDERICK

Go at it like Indiana Jones.

The message bubbles appeared and disappeared for a moment, so I held off replying. When the message came through, I wanted to cry.

FREDERICK

Thank you so much, sweetheart. You're really saving me here. I'll make sure to bring you a gift.

REN

Free time with a puppy? I think I'm the one who's lucked out.

Not to mention that I now had some breathing space in my search for a room.

By the time my shift at the store finished, I was dying for a shower and food. I almost panicked when I forgot about the key to Frederick's apartment, but then I remembered he'd given me a copy so I could come see my succulents while he was away during the summer.

I retrieved it from the glovebox—it was hidden in a little pouch—and drove to Frederick's place where my new roomie waited for me.

Frederick

I stared at the white blanket of snow outside. We were definitely going to have a white Christmas. If I wasn't so worried for Ren, I'd welcome the postcard picture in front of my window.

Instead, all I could think about was the passing of time and how I was running out of excuses to keep Ren with me.

The fake work trip I'd taken was me checking into a hotel where I'd hidden for the best part of a week in case I accidentally bumped into Ren.

He'd sent me photos of himself with the puppy he'd named Melon by the Christmas tree we'd decorated the weekend before and promised to stock my fridge before I returned home.

I wouldn't have cared if he'd eaten every bit of food in my fridge. The puppy was a rescue from the animal shelter, and since he was too young to be with the other dogs, the shelter had been looking for someone to foster him until he could be adopted.

I decided to keep the puppy for good when I received the first photo of the dog asleep on Ren's lap. His smile as he stared at the dog was pure love.

I'd emailed the paperwork to the shelter and had dropped by during the week to finalize the adoption.

Melon came barreling into the bedroom, jumping at my feet.

"Hello, you heathen. Are you finished helping your daddy in the kitchen?"

Melon yipped his reply, and I stroked his short caramel-colored coat. He was wearing a collar with Christmas decorations hanging from it. It made me smile because it was so Ren.

"You've gotta stop saying that," Ren said from the door. The dog ran back to him, asking to be picked up, which Ren obliged.

"Saying what?"

"That I'm his daddy. It'll be hard enough to give him back to Emery. How long are they away anyway?"

I bit my lip. There were already too many lies between us. This one didn't need to exist.

"Actually, I have a confession," I said.

Ren walked in and sat on my bed with Melon on his lap.

"Melon is actually yours."

He looked at Melon and then at me. "He is?"

I sat next to them on the bed. "You mentioned before about having a dog growing up and how you'd love to have another one. I figured Melon could live here with me, and you'll see him often enough."

Ren's lower lip trembled. "I don't know what to say. This is the nicest thing anyone's ever done for me."

I pulled him closer, and Melon put his front legs on mine so he could lay across Ren and me. "You deserve all the nice things, Ren. I would give you the world if I knew you'd take it."

Ren's big brown eyes were on me, shiny with unshed tears. When he blinked, one fell down his cheek.

His breath caught when I cleared the tear away with my thumb. God, he was so beautiful. He leaned a little closer, his eyes moving between mine and my mouth. I licked my lower lip, frozen in place, waiting for what was coming next.

I wouldn't stop it. Dammit. If Ren put his lips on mine, that would be it for us. No more sleeping anywhere else but my bed, no more going hungry to save money for the store. Not that Ren had ever let me believe he was saving on food to put the money away, but he was stubborn enough to do it.

When he leaned forward, I closed my eyes until his lips landed on my cheek.

"Thank you so much, Frederick. One day, I'll repay you for all your kindness."

He may as well have thrown me down the garbage shoot with the rest of the trash. Or dunked me in an ice bath.

The evidence that we weren't on the same page was clear. I was just a friend. A friend whom Ren felt he had to repay things to that real friends never did. Which meant I wasn't even best-friend material.

"So what's for dinner then? You told me to stay away

from the kitchen. Do I need to call the fire department?" I asked, trying to keep the disappointment from my voice.

He cleared his throat. "Um, it's nearly ready. Give me just ten minutes, and then you can come out."

Melon jumped to the carpet when Ren stood and followed him to the kitchen, no doubt hoping to get some scraps of whatever was making my apartment smell like a Michelin-star restaurant.

I stood and went over to the window again. There was no reason to feel hurt, but I did. Rejection sucked, even when the other person was unaware of it.

I just had to think of Ren. My friend, Ren.

While I was away, Ren's messages were always happy, teasing, and like he was his usual happy self. He'd taken a selfie in my bed, threatening to take over my whole bedroom if I didn't come home. I'd wanted to say that he should stay there instead of in his room, preferably with clothes off, and not leave until I could join him.

It was just wishful thinking. Even if I'd been in a position to say it, I was afraid I'd be too scared to do something. Ren wasn't the first man I'd been attracted to, but while I'd dismissed the others as a fluke result of being a horny teenager, it was different with Ren.

I wanted to run my tongue over the smooth skin of his stomach. The skin that teased me every time he was in my home wearing nothing but those tiny sleep shorts and crop tops.

I wanted to run my hands all over his body, knead the globes of his perfect butt with my eager hands, and find out if he tasted like mint all the time or only after he'd brushed his teeth.

A week in a hotel room with nothing but work and thoughts of Ren had been torture...for the housekeeper too. I was sure she could tell exactly how many times I'd made myself come. She probably thought my hotel room had a revolving door of sex partners.

When I couldn't stay at the hotel any longer, I'd come home to Ren cuddled on the couch with Melon, watching the lights on the Christmas tree.

Even though I knew nothing would ever happen between us, I liked having Ren in my space. I craved it and couldn't imagine coming home and him not being here. How screwed up was that?

After my "business trip," I'd "caught the flu," so Ren had offered to stay longer to look after me. When I could no longer pretend to be sick, or he'd march me down to the hospital, I'd had a miraculous recovery. But then there was a Christmas concert we had to go to, and a new Christmas movie came out in the theaters, so we went to the movies.

Of course, all these nights, it was better if Ren stayed with me instead of driving back to his parents' house.

I saw the relief in his eyes every time there was a legitimate reason to stay.

And every day, my torture increased.

I'd never taken so many showers or used them so often to relieve the sexual tension of being around Ren. I was at a stage where I wasn't sure if my apartment smelled like him or if he'd been here so long that he smelled like my apartment.

Yesterday, we'd bumped into each other as he'd come out of the bathroom after a shower with only a tiny towel wrapped around his waist.

My mouth had watered at the sight of his tiny dark nipples and the trail of light hair that disappeared under the towel.

I swear I drooled. How Ren didn't suspect I was attracted to him, I didn't know. Then again, if all he saw in me was a friend, he'd never see beyond that.

"Dinner's ready. You may come out," Ren shouted from the kitchen.

I went from the bedroom into the kitchen, but neither Ren nor our dinner was on the table. Since the kitchen had two archway entries, one to the hallway leading to the bedrooms and one to the living room, I went through to the living room.

"Surprise!"

The Christmas tree lights were turned on, the TV displayed a fireplace with burning logs and sound, and Ren was sitting on the floor in front of the couch. The coffee table had been pushed aside, and he'd put a picnic blanket over the carpet.

"What's this?"

"It's a Christmas picnic, of course."

I chuckled and sat on the floor next to Ren. He handed me a bowl filled with the most delicious-looking ziti.

Melon was by the tree chewing on a toy. No doubt Ren had bribed him with dinner before our dinner to ensure he didn't jump on ours.

"This looks amazing, Ren. Thank you."

He blushed, reached for a bottle of wine, and poured us each a glass.

I tried the ziti, moaning when I tasted the first bite.

"Oh my god, this is amazing. It tastes exactly like the one from the restaurant by the river."

He broke into a grin. "That's because I used the same recipe."

"How? I doubt the chef gave it to you."

He shrugged. "I've been watching him for months and making notes. I figured if I could make the ziti like he does, I could convince him to let me work in the kitchen sometimes. They make more money than the servers."

I took another bite. "He'd be silly not to hire you. Unless he thinks you're competition. I'll be honest. If you opened a restaurant just making this ziti, you'd have a golden goose on your hands.

"Nah. I just want my flower shop, that's all."

Frederick was crazy if he thought I'd be any good at running a food business.

Flowers were my jam. I had countless sketchbooks with designs for wedding arrangements, birthday bouquets, proposals, engagement parties, you name it.

I'd practiced a lot when I worked in my ex's parents' store and always took photos of my work. They never liked me experimenting with new designs or mixing flowers they didn't approve of, but if a client gave me free rein, I'd give them the best flower arrangement they could afford.

We ate the ziti and drank the wine mostly in silence. Frederick's moans were too loud, and every single one went straight to my groin.

I hoped he hadn't noticed how I'd pulled a cushion from the couch onto my lap.

"Okay, so what are we watching tonight?" I asked, placing the empty food bowl on the blanket and stretching my legs out.

Frederick reached for the remote control.

"I'm finding this fireplace to be somewhat faulty in the way it doesn't produce any heat."

I chuckled.

"So, I thought we might want to watch a documentary called Flora of the Pacific Northwest, based on the manual first published in 1973."

My mouth gaped in astonishment.

"Did you know I have a copy of the original book?" I asked, wondering if he'd seen it among my stuff.

"You do?"

I nodded.

"I didn't know, but I figured you'd like to watch the documentary as they show every flower, plant, and tree listed in the book."

The knot stuck in my throat since Frederick had told me he'd adopted Melon for me was getting tighter and tighter.

Making dinner for Frederick paled compared to how much he'd done for me in the last couple of weeks. Well, months, if I counted the fact he'd happily taken in all my succulents.

They'd thrived under his care, and he'd even tried to propagate some, saying he wanted to keep his own after I opened my store and started selling my current ones.

Being around Frederick was dangerous for my heart and my body.

Today, I'd almost kissed him, and yesterday, I'd almost been bold enough to drop the towel after my shower just to gauge his reaction.

And it was exactly because his reactions to me were becoming increasingly confusing that I needed to not be around him.

My obsession gave me ideas I shouldn't entertain. It built stories and hopes in my head that would never have a place in real life.

Frederick pressed play on the documentary, so I pushed my thoughts aside.

Melon stopped playing with his toy and came to sit on my lap.

The documentary was practically porn to me. I kept reaching for my phone to make notes about flowers I wanted to learn more about.

But the inevitability of my situation was never far from the front of my mind.

"What has you thinking so hard?" Frederick asked, running his fingers through my hair. At some point, he must have leaned back against the couch and draped his arm over the seat. "I thought you'd enjoy watching this."

"I am enjoying it. I just have other things on my mind."

"Anything I can do to help?"

I sighed. "No." I could tell from how his fingers paused on my head that he wanted to challenge me. He wanted to help because that's what he always did.

"Fine. I can't be here forever, and I need a place to live in the city. I've been looking, but so far, nothing has come up. I think it's because it's so close to Christmas." At least, that was what the last realtor I'd spoken to said. People will wait to move after the holidays, so there should be more availability in January.

"Why do you need a new place?" he asked.

"Because it's too exhausting to travel back and forth all the time." *Not to mention sleeping in the car when it's so cold.*

He was quiet for a moment. "How about you stay here for good?"

"What?" I reached for the remote control and paused the documentary. "No. I can't do that."

He furrowed his brows. "Why?"

"Because..." I struggled to find a good enough reason. "Because...um...I don't want to be in your way, and I'm sure I can't afford rent in a place like this."

"Why do you think you'd be in the way? Have I made you feel like that over the last two weeks?"

He sounded hurt. I rubbed my eyes and took a deep breath.

"You haven't made me feel anything but welcome, Frederick. That's the problem."

"How is that a problem?"

"Because I like it here too much, but what happens when you want to bring a girl over? You won't want your gay friend as a third wheel."

He opened his mouth and then closed it again. See? You couldn't argue with that logic.

"Have you seen any girls here?" he asked.

"No, but—"

"Precisely. I'm focused on my work and have no desire to date women right now."

Yeah, but it would happen at some point. The point where I'd have made a home here with Melon, and it would break my heart to move out.

That's what I should have said. What came out instead was, "I can't afford it."

"Yes, you can," he said.

"Excuse me? How do you know what I can and can't afford?"

This conversation was making me anxious, and I didn't even know why. I stood, grabbed our plates, and took them to the kitchen. When I returned for the empty wine glasses, Frederick grabbed my hand.

I plopped onto the ground in front of him.

"The rent for this place is ridiculously cheap. The owner is a family friend who bought this as an investment. He doesn't need the rental income, so this is practically free. If you want, you can contribute toward the utilities, and I'll cover the rent."

"Can I think about it?"

"Sure."

I stood again, cleared the rest of the stuff from dinner, and put the coffee table back in its place.

"I think I'll go to bed now. I have an early start tomorrow."

"Ren," Frederick called. He stood and stopped in front of me.

My heart pounded in confusion, want, and god knew how many other feelings.

"Never mind," he said.

"I'll stop by after work to pick up my stuff. I should go back home, right?"

"Please stay. Just until you make up your mind."

I sighed and nodded.

"Goodnight, Frederick."

"Goodnight, sweetheart."

Rule number one: *if* I was to stay and rent the room I'd been using for months, he had to stop calling me that.

I tossed and turned all night. It was frustrating and exhausting. Even Melon, who'd gotten used to sleeping at my feet, at some point left the bedroom and probably went to snuggle with Frederick.

I wasn't sad. Not one bit. I was also not lying to myself and was totally not jealous of a puppy.

Deep down, I knew I couldn't take Frederick's offer, so with that resolve, I forced myself to sleep.

When I got up in the morning, noises were coming from the kitchen and I smelled coffee and eggs.

"Morning," I said. "What are you doing up so early?"

Frederick usually walked to work, which took him twenty minutes. I never saw him this early.

"I couldn't sleep, and I had an idea," he said, pointing to the table where he'd put cups of coffee and a couple of plates with scrambled eggs and toast.

"Okay?"

"I know why you don't want to stay here."

"You do?"

"Yes. Look, I get it. You want to feel like you've earned your independence. I know how it feels. I've worked hard for my independence from my parents too. I think what you're doing to get your store is the bravest thing I've ever seen anyone do. Everyone I know had everything handed to them without questions. You're working for it, and you don't want to feel like you're being given handouts."

I didn't have an answer to that. His insight was extremely...insightful.

"Thank you. You're right. So you understand why I can't stay."

He smiled. "I do, but...I need your help with something, and I was wondering if we could come to an agreement."

"What do you need?"

"My parents are going to Europe for Christmas, so they've invited me and my boyfriend to spend next weekend with them in a kind of early Christmas celebration."

I coughed. "I'm sorry, you and your what?"

"My boyfriend. You remember I lied to my mom years ago about being gay so she would stop setting me up with her friends' daughters?"

I nodded.

"Well, since I 'broke it off with Emery,'" he said in air quotes, "I didn't have the heart to tell them the truth."

"So they still think you're gay?"

He nodded. "And they think you're my boyfriend."

I raised my brows. "Come again?"

"I guess I talked about you so much, they just assumed. Would you come with me next weekend and be my fake boyfriend?"

Well, shit.

Frederick

I've *fucked it up. I've fucked it up.*

What the hell went through my mind that I'd ask Ren to be my fake boyfriend? Hadn't I already played that game with Emery? And look what happened? He fell in love with someone else.

Would Ren also fall in love with someone else?

Was I cursed?

In the middle of my mental breakdown, I realized Ren was staring at me like a deer in headlights.

"Say something..."

He laughed. "What do you want me to say? That it's the most ridiculous idea I've ever heard? Do you really think your parents would believe you and I are together?"

The comment hurt. "Why wouldn't they?"

"Because...because you're you, and I'm...me." He pointed at himself. All I saw was perfection, but this wasn't the time to point it out.

"They'll believe whatever we tell them. Besides, we know each other well enough that we can pass."

"I'm not sure. I don't like to lie."

"It's not a lie. We're friends, and we know each other really well by now. I can recite all your favorite foods and which clothes you like wearing when you go grocery shopping. I even know they're different if you go window shopping. I know what you want the most in life. I know you know me too."

Could he read the despair in my voice? It wasn't lying. My parents had invited me and the man I'd mentioned so many times that they'd made an assumption. While I hadn't accepted their invite yet, I also hadn't declined it.

"Is it just the weekend?" he asked.

"Yes. I promise."

"Do we have to sleep together?"

"No. There are plenty of rooms in the house. You can pick one next to mine, and they'll never know."

"Okay," he said.

"So you'll let me repay you by moving in here?"

He sighed. "Yes, but I want to see those utility bills, and I want to pay them myself if you refuse to take any rent."

"Deal." *Not a chance.* I'd work on avoiding the topic later. I'd seen the battle inside him. He didn't want to move out but couldn't tell me he'd been sleeping in his car. I hated that his pride was getting in the way of his safety and well-being. But I hated myself more for not asking him to move in months ago after he'd started staying over regularly during the weekends.

We finished our breakfast, and I offered to do the dishes

since I didn't need to be at work for another couple of hours.

After Ren left for work, I fed Melon and played with him for a bit. He fell asleep on my lap. I knew exactly how he felt. Sadly, I still had a day of work ahead of me.

"No naps for Frederick, right?"

He did a big stretch and moved his paws like he was chasing something.

"I hope you're having a nice dream, buddy."

I leaned back on the couch but was too afraid I'd fall asleep, so I got up after settling Melon on his bed in the living room and went to my room.

It's funny how when you're having fun, two hours fly past, but when you have two hours to kill, you literally wish you had something to kill to make time go faster.

I started a load of laundry and changed my sheets. I wondered if I should do Ren's too, but it wouldn't be right to invade the privacy of his bedroom, even though most of the time he left his door open, even when he was asleep.

Emery called just as I brewed another cup of coffee.

"Hey, how's things?" I asked.

"You tell me."

"Huh?"

"Why did Ren call me asking what your parents are like, if they'd give your new boyfriend a hard time, even at Christmas, and if he should buy them a gift?"

I groaned. "Because I'm a jackass thinking with his dick instead of his brain."

"What do you mean? And by the way, be quick. I'm

almost at the school, so I can't swear once I'm through the gates."

I told Emery everything. From the lies I'd told Ren to get him to move into my apartment to the ridiculous plan to have him as my fake boyfriend for Christmas with my family.

"Okay, so while I don't condone the lying, I agree Ren shouldn't sleep in his car. Sometimes I can't believe he's the same man who threw a bunch of grapefruit at Lex and me when he was mad at his ex."

I chuckled. That had been the night I'd been summoned to keep an eye on Ren.

"I know I shouldn't do the whole fake-boyfriend thing again, but I didn't know what to do. He seems to be under the impression that he has to pay people back for all the nice things they do for him. I knew unless he had to do a big favor, he'd feel like a charity case when it came to moving in for good."

"Can you fake it?" Emery asked.

I sighed. "That's the problem, Em. I won't need to fake it."

"I don't know what to tell you, hun. I love you both, and I'm scared you'll both end up hurt. I'm not entirely sure Ren doesn't have feelings for you."

"What—what?"

"Oh dear lord. How can you be so blind to it? You two have practically been dating for months. You're the one he turns to when he's stuck. Not to mention that simply speaking your name makes him blush like a virgin maiden from a regency novel."

Was that true? Surely I'd have noticed? Or had I been so blind because I'd convinced myself Ren would never see me as anything but a straight man and a friend?

"Your silence tells me you're either freaking out or having a rare moment of clarity," Emery said.

I laughed. "Maybe a bit of both."

"Good. Listen to your gut and pay attention to Ren. What he doesn't say with his loud mouth, he says loudly with his body language."

Emery ended the call because he'd arrived at work, which reminded me I needed to go too. I left enough food and water for Melon and made my way through the cool December morning to the office.

I kept Emery's words in mind the whole way. If he was right, then maybe I had a chance with Ren. I just needed to figure out a way to come out to him without making him run scared.

When Ren messaged me later that day telling me not to worry about dinner for him because he was finishing work late and could fix himself a sandwich, I made a decision.

The man I was in love with deserved a nice meal at the end of the day. There was no way I'd let him just have a sandwich. Not unless it was a grilled cheese and came with a nice bowl of tomato soup.

I also needed a new plan.

Ren

Frederick had been acting weird since the day I'd gotten home late and he'd made me soup and a grilled cheese. I'd caught him staring at me a few times, which he'd played off by saying I had something in my hair or that he was just distracted. It had put me on edge over the weekend. I'd been someone's secret boyfriend, but never a fake one.

The problem wasn't even faking it. The problem was what would happen if I believed my own lies and fell even harder for him.

How could I handle him touching me like we were together and not believe it was true? Surely, he wouldn't go heavy on the PDA in front of his parents, right?

It was with all these conflicted emotions and very shaky hands that I got in Frederick's car on Friday after he picked me up from work.

I'd given him strict instructions to not forget my clothes

bag and to carefully pack the pot of succulents I'd put together as a gift for his mom.

Thankfully, I knew someone who worked at the gym across from the grocery store, and she let me shower and change there after work, so at least I wouldn't meet Frederick's mom smelling like a grocery store.

"You look nervous," he said as I buckled my seatbelt.

"I'm meeting my fake boyfriend's parents. Nervous doesn't even cover it. I'm terrified."

Frederick put a hand on my knee and looked me in the eyes. "It's going to be okay."

I scoffed. "Emery said your parents are old-money rich. They'll probably have a hundred pieces of cutlery just for breakfast. I'll never pass like I belong, let alone fit in."

"You'll be with me, so I'll help you with any cutlery issues that may arise."

"Don't joke," I chided.

"I'm not. And I don't want you to fit in, Ren. It's because you're you that I like you."

His words settled me a little but didn't push all my anxiety away.

My anxiety multiplied by a bazillion when, less than an hour later, we approached Frederick's parents' castle.

Okay, so it wasn't a castle as such, but it may as well be. The house was huge, and there were smaller houses on either side. Was it all the same? Surely, if you had a house that big, you wouldn't have neighbors that close.

"Oh my god, you have to turn back." I put my shaky hand on Frederick's arm.

"Why?"

"Why? Why? Have you seen the size of that house?"

He laughed. "I believe so. I grew up in it, after all. There are plenty of hiding places if you ever need to escape."

He winked. He fucking winked. Maybe this was a joke to him, but I didn't want to let him down. I wanted his parents to like me, even though I couldn't understand why that was important to me.

"Come on, let's get inside before they send someone out to get us."

We got out of the car, and Frederick insisted on taking both our bags while I carried the succulent pot.

The front door opened as we approached. I wondered if it had a sensor when I saw an older woman dressed as a maid come through.

"Mrs. Jensen," Frederick said, placing the bags on the marbled floor and giving the woman a hug.

"Welcome back, my dear. We missed you. I don't know what's got into your momma, but all she talks about these days is you. You'd never hear the end of it if you mentioned it, but I think she missed you."

"I missed everyone too. I promise not to go so long between visits. I've just been preoccupied with work, that's all."

The woman looked at him from head to toe like she was assessing him before she seemed to decide he was all right. Then she turned to me.

"And this must be your beau. Ren, is it?"

I nodded and held out my hand. "Pleasure to meet you."

The woman pushed my hand away and pulled me for a hug.

Frederick laughed. "There are no formalities with Mrs. Jensen. She's worked for the family since I was in diapers, so nothing gets past her."

My eyes widened. Would she know about us?

"Come on, let's find Mom," Frederick said.

"I'll take these to your room, my dear," Mrs. Jensen said.

I panicked. "Oh, um, we won't be sleeping together."

"Why not? This is an old house, but I can assure you, my dear, we're not old-fashioned."

"But—"

"Besides, there's a big redecorating project going on. You're lucky Frederick's room is the last one, or you'd have to sleep in the guesthouse."

"That's fine, Mrs. Jensen. We'll sleep in my room. Do you know where Mom is?"

"She was picking out Christmas decorations earlier in the drawing room."

Frederick held my hand and pulled me farther into the huge foyer. Is it even called a foyer when you could fit my parents' house inside?

The floors were marble throughout, double stairs led to the second floor, and there were flowers everywhere. I liked them. They calmed me.

I tried to take in as much as I could. "Please never leave me alone in this house. I'll get lost, and you'll find me withered into a sad skeleton from lack of food and water."

"Don't worry, baby. I'll always find you, and I'll make

sure to carry extra snacks and drinks wherever we go."

"My hero." I swooned while my brain was going *What the fuck? Did he just call me baby?*

We found Frederick's mom practically buried under piles of boxes, all labeled *Christmas Decorations*. Each box had a year on it.

"Frederick, my dear, you're here," she said, coming around the boxes. I expected her to hug Frederick first, but she came straight to me, giving me an awkward but tight hug.

"And you must be Laurence, right? Frederick says you go by Ren, but I love your full name so much. May I call you Laurence?"

"Of course. It's a pleasure to meet you, Mrs. Rhys-Myr. This is for you." I held out the pot. "It's from my succulent collection."

"Oh wow, they're beautiful. Frederick says you're somewhat of a flower expert."

My cheeks warmed under her praise. "Um, yeah, I love flowers."

"Do you have a flower store or something? My usual florist is retiring, and it's becoming an impossible task to find someone who understands what I need."

I glanced at Frederick, but he just shrugged.

"No. I don't have a flower store. I'm sort of saving money to open one." *Great, and now she knows you're poor.*

Not that there was anything wrong with being poor. I was very proud of my achievements, but I didn't want Frederick's parents to look down on me because I wasn't a successful business owner yet.

"Frederick." She gave her son a light smack on his arm. "Why haven't you helped your lovely boyfriend open his business? What's that fancy business degree for? Surely not just to make the Livingstons richer, is it?"

"Mom," Frederick sighed. "This is not our business."

"Of course, but there's no harm in a little help, right?"

I pushed through a smile. "I appreciate the sentiment, Mrs. Rhys-Myr, but this is something I'm doing on my own. Sure, it'll take me a little longer, but I want to know that when it happens, it's because I made it happen."

She broke into a wide smile. "Frederick, hold on to this one."

"I will, Mom," Frederick said, pulling me closer until his arm was around my shoulder. Then he kissed the top of my head.

Stop beating so fast, you stupid heart.

"Why don't you two go freshen up before dinner," she suggested before returning to the boxes.

Frederick pulled me out of the room and up the stairs. We passed at least ten closed doors before we stopped in front of one with a wooden plaque that said *Freddy's Room.*

"So there *is* someone other than Winnie who calls you Freddy," I joked.

He laughed. "Nope. They just couldn't find one with Frederick." He opened the door, and we walked inside.

Frederick stayed by the door while I went all the way in.

"Your room is at least twice the size of my childhood bedroom. It's a shame it's already dark. I guess I'll see what kind of view you have from here tomorrow."

"I think you'll like it."

I turned to face Frederick.

"What?"

"You're the first boyfriend I've ever had in my bedroom."

I rolled my eyes. "Probably the last too."

"If I have anything to say about that, you will be."

My stomach tightened. He meant he wouldn't be bringing any other fake boyfriends over. He'd be bringing girls. That was it. He didn't mean what my ears heard and misinterpreted.

Both our bags were on the bed. I looked at my tatty old bag compared to Frederick's nice new one, and panic suddenly overcame me.

"Fuck." I opened the bag and rummaged around.

"What's up? Did you forget something?"

"Yeah, something to sleep in. I usually sleep in just my underwear. I didn't think we'd be sleeping together."

"How about those nice pajamas you have?"

I shook my head. "I didn't bring them because I didn't think I needed them. Usually, I take them off before going to sleep."

Frederick went over to the dresser and opened the top drawer.

"Here. Try this."

I took the shirt he handed me. It looked and smelled new and expensive. It was also huge, but it would have to do.

"Thank you."

"Okay, now that's solved, let's go downstairs for dinner. Dad is usually in the office until dinner time. He doesn't chill until after dinner, and he always goes to bed late."

Dinner with Frederick's parents was surprisingly normal. I could tell they loved their son, even if his mom's obsession with him settling down was a little too much.

I'd nearly choked on a piece of bread when she brought up the topic of children. Mine and Frederick's children, to be precise.

I hadn't lied when I said I'd love to have children after I opened my store and was settled financially. Frederick hadn't said anything, but he'd looked at me in a way I couldn't quite figure out.

The worst part of dinner was that Frederick insisted on having his hand on my leg. At some point, his little finger was perilously close to my dick, which had been hard throughout.

I tried to keep calm and breathe through it, but when enough was enough, I excused myself and went up to his room. If it hadn't had the plaque with his name on it, there was no way I'd have found it.

When I got inside, I closed the door behind me and locked myself inside the attached bathroom.

I washed my face with cold water and willed my dick to stand down. I refused to jerk one out in Frederick's childhood bedroom. It was wrong on too many levels.

Frederick was sitting on the bed when I came out with my teeth already brushed.

"You okay?"

"Yeah, I just thought something from dinner didn't agree with me, but it was a false alarm."

"Okay." He grabbed his bag and went into the bathroom.

I took the opportunity to change from my clothes into the T-shirt I'd borrowed from him. Before he came out, I got into bed and hid under the covers.

When the light in the bathroom turned off, I closed my eyes. I could not see Frederick in his underwear, or I'd for sure have an orgasm right here.

The light in the bedroom stayed off, so the only light came from the hallway outside. I heard scrabbling noises and a couple of muffled swear words before the bed dipped beside me.

"Are you asleep?" he whispered.

"No."

"I'm glad you're here, Ren."

I smiled to myself in the dark. Despite everything, I'd enjoyed meeting Frederick's family and seeing a different side to him.

"Me too."

There was nothing but silence for a while.

"If you snore, I'll kick you out of bed," I said.

"The future father of your children? You wouldn't?"

"Oh, I would."

I could swear I heard him smile. "I won't snore. Promise."

"Night, Freddy."

"Night, my love."

Be still, my little beating heart. He's just staying in the role. Be still.

Frederick

I slept surprisingly well, considering that when I'd first gotten into bed with Ren, it had taken Superman-level willpower not to confess everything right there and pull him into my arms.

I'd woken a few times during the night when Ren had muttered something in his sleep. It was hard to understand at first, but after a while, I got it. He was reciting the Latin names of what I assumed to be flowers.

It was so adorable that I'd turned to face him and just watched as his brows furrowed when he was thinking of a name and then smoothed out when he got it.

I must have fallen asleep in that position and then turned on my back because when I woke in the morning, with the sun coming through the gap in the curtains, that's how I was. The only difference was that Ren had gravitated toward me and was completely wrapped around my body.

I didn't know how he'd managed to get one of his legs under mine, but aside from the painful erection trapped under his other leg, I liked being his personal snuggle pillow.

He'd also managed to get his hand under my T-shirt and rest it on my chest over my heart.

All week, I'd been doing what Emery advised. I'd watched Ren.

I found that he spent a lot of time staring at me, specifically my ass.

It was funny the things you noticed when you were looking for them. The backsplash in my kitchen was the perfect accomplice because it helped me watch Ren without him noticing.

We'd shared chores, working easily around each other. I'd listened as he sang to his plants when he didn't think I was watching, but it was the conversations he had that were more telling.

If the succulents could talk, I wondered if they'd give away Ren's secrets or have some kind of loyalty to their main parent.

On Thursday, when I'd been packing for the weekend, I'd needed to get something from the laundry room, so I'd accidentally snuck up on him talking to his succulents again.

"Please give me strength to remember this whole thing is fake. He's not mine and never will be," he'd whispered.

I'd walked away with a huge smile, almost forgetting what I had meant to pick up from the laundry room.

I should've told him then how I felt, that I was already his and had been for the longest time, but I'd chickened out. Now, all I could do was count the minutes until we were back in our apartment, in the privacy of our walls, before I could tell him.

Ren let out a sleepy sigh, and I couldn't resist turning my head to smell his hair. Okay, this was wrong, and I knew I shouldn't do it, but he was the one who'd come to me in his sleep. I was only human, after all.

When his hand slid over my chest and tickled my armpit, I trembled.

Suddenly, I was staring at a very wide-eyed Ren. Still half-asleep but already in panic mode. It took him a few seconds to work out exactly what was going on and that he was the one holding on to me. It was as clear on his face as the light from the snow-covered morning outside.

"Morning," I said.

He scrambled to his side of the bed, pulling the covers over his shoulders.

"Oh my god, Frederick. I'm so sorry. I...this is so embarrassing."

I turned to him. "It's okay."

"No, it's not. I wouldn't want to wake up to a girl rubbing herself all over me, so I get that this is totally inappropriate. I can get dressed quickly and give you privacy to grab a shower to get my smell off you."

He started to scramble off the bed, but I held him by the waist and pulled him closer. He was so tense I swear he'd snap in two at the slightest trigger.

"First of all, it's okay. You were asleep, so you can't be blamed for wanting to be closer to this hot body." I winked. "And second, you smell nice. You smell like my body wash and your cologne. I like it."

His Adam's apple bobbed, and I wanted nothing more than to bite it and lick a path up his neck until I could close my lips over his.

"Frederick, don't mess with me," he pleaded.

"I wouldn't think of it, sweetheart."

"Fred—" He started to protest, but I shut him up by kissing his forehead.

"Come on, let's get up, or Mom will send out a search party if we're not down for breakfast."

He groaned. "You go first."

I obliged because the bathroom was on my side of the bed. I could go without revealing how hard I was for Ren, and it would give him time to get his morning wood under control too.

I grabbed a quick shower, not so much to get his smell off me because I'd gladly wear him all day. I needed to cool down.

A sudden bout of nerves hit me. What if I couldn't... perform? I'd never been with a man before. I knew what I liked, and I'd been curious enough to watch gay porn, but I knew real life would be a lot different. What if I couldn't make it good for Ren?

"Stop it. You're getting ahead of yourself," I said to myself. I turned the water off and dried myself with the towel.

Realizing I hadn't brought clean clothes into the bath-room, I walked into the bedroom with just the towel around my waist.

"Jesus Christ, Frederick," Ren groaned.

"I guess we're even now," I said, grabbing my bag from

the floor to pick something to wear as he scurried into the bathroom.

Ren came out fifteen minutes later, fully dressed and looking ready to face whatever was thrown at him.

Mom was in the kitchen, nursing a cup of her favorite breakfast tea, while Mrs. Jensen put some pastries on a plate.

"Morning, boys," Mrs. Jensen said.

"Morning."

"Morning, honey," Mom said as I kissed her cheek.

I grabbed a couple of cups and filled them with coffee. For all the formalities of living in a house big enough to have staff, breakfast was probably the most normal thing we did.

Mrs. Jensen always joined us for breakfast before she went on with her day managing the household, and we just picked whatever we wanted from what was on offer.

I picked a couple of pastries and brought them to Ren with our coffee.

"Thank you. This looks really good," he said.

"Thank you, my dear," Mrs. Jensen said. "I don't want to brag, but since I took a pastry class last year, our breakfasts have gone up a notch."

"As has my waistline," Mom complained, even as she grabbed a pastry.

"So what's in store for today, Mom?"

She shared a look with Mrs. Jensen. "We have a dinner party tonight. Don't worry." She raised her hand before I said anything. "It's only for close friends. The Livingstons are coming. Lex and Emery too. And a few friends from the club."

Next to me, Ren tensed. "Mom, I thought it was going to be just us."

She waved me off. "And a few carefully chosen friends. Besides, I want them to meet Ren."

I sighed, reaching under the table for Ren's hand.

"When you finish breakfast, you can show Ren the garden, and then after lunch, we can decorate the Christmas tree."

She stood and left the kitchen.

"She drops the bomb and runs," I groaned.

"Frederick, that's no way to talk about your mother," Mrs. Jensen chided.

Ren giggled. I'd take being scolded by the housekeeper any day just to hear Ren laugh.

"Come on, finish your breakfast so we can go outside."

It had been a while since I'd seen the garden under such a beautiful blanket of snow. The only downside was that it was really cold, but I'd found my old winter coats.

Ren was adoringly drowning in the smallest one I had. His nose was pink from the cold and he had a woolly hat that covered his hair and ears.

"How was it growing up here?" he asked.

"I was...sometimes oppressive, but not too bad."

"Oppressive?"

I tried to find the right words to explain. "I went to a private school, so I had no frame of reference for the outside world. Everyone I knew had money, and a lot of the kids were spoiled brats. I wanted to experience the stuff I saw on TV. Kids going to the mall to watch a movie and birthday parties that didn't involve an event planner."

"I can see that. You never come across as someone with lots of money," Ren said.

"That's because I don't have lots of money. My parents do. I mean, I have a trust fund I barely use, but I prefer living off what I make from my job."

Ren wrapped his arms around mine, and we walked side by side. He pointed out all the various trees and plants we had, impressed by how some survived the cold.

By the time we went back inside, we both needed a hot drink.

"Oh, boys, there you are," Mom said when she found us in the kitchen huddled in front of the coffee maker, willing it to brew the coffee quicker. "Ren, I need your help."

Ren looked at me. I nodded.

"Sure. What can I do?"

Ren

It was a surreal experience to be asked by the most sophisticated woman I'd ever met to help her pick out the decorations for her Christmas tree. Especially when she had a dinner party to host in the evening.

This was the perfect distraction from obsessing over how Frederick seemed to have changed in the last twenty-four hours. He was touchy-feely with me. More than usual. The terms of endearment were more frequent, and this morning?

I thought he was going to kiss me. The way he'd looked at me had been intense, with razor-sharp focus.

Men didn't go from being straight one day to gay the next. I had to remember that. He liked me as a friend, and we were in each other's space so much that it was natural to have some intimacy.

"What are your colors for the party?" I asked Frederick's mom as I followed her along the hallways.

"We don't really have any this time. You see, my

husband sprung this trip on me, so when I would usually be speaking to my event planner and decorator, I was busy making travel arrangements. I pushed all the Christmas stuff aside.”

“How about traditional Christmas colors? Greens, reds, gold, or silver?” I suggested.

She opened a set of double doors that took us to a large dining room with a table that could easily seat twenty people or more.

Various people were busy bringing things inside the room from another entrance. I noticed the tablecloth was white.

“Do you have a table runner?” I asked.

“We do, somewhere.” She opened a few boxes before letting out a victorious yes. “Red and green.”

“Perfect. We can match the tree to that if you have enough decorations.”

She laughed, pointing at the boxes.

Frederick joined us but sat on a couch in the living area next to the seven-foot-tall Christmas tree.

For the next two hours, we checked all the boxes for the best decorations that matched the color scheme. I noticed a box that was unopened and asked about it.

“Those are decorations Frederick made when he was a child.”

“Can I see them?”

“No,” Frederick shouted. “Yes,” his mom said at the same time.

I opened the box like it was a treasure chest containing Frederick’s secrets. The essence of who he was.

Inside were dozens of decorations. Some were hand-made using a milk carton or a toilet paper roll, but others were painted-glass decorations.

"I think these should go on the tree," I said.

"But they don't match the color scheme," his mom said.

"Please forgive me if I'm stepping out of line, Mrs. Rhys-Myr, but Christmas is about family. Even though you won't be here for Christmas, you're still taking the time to get your family and friends together. It shouldn't be just about the food and color-coordinated decorations. The soul of your family is in this box. You should put it all on display."

She thought about it for a moment before she grabbed one of the decorations from the box. "I remember this one. You made it at school. You were so proud of it and wanted it on the tree that year," she said, sitting next to Frederick. "It never went on the tree because it didn't match anything, but I think Laurence is right. All of these should be out."

For a moment, I'd thought she would kick me out of her house for disrespecting her, but instead, I found myself on the receiving end of a mom hug and thanks.

Frederick helped us pick where the decorations went on the tree, and at the end, before we turned the lights on, he picked me up and ordered me to place the star on top.

I choked a little. The last time I'd put a star on a Christmas tree was the year Winnie was born. After that, she'd always gotten to do it, and I'd never noticed how much I'd missed that simple thing.

"Thank you," I whispered as I hugged him.

"No. Thank *you* for giving me a real Christmas with my parents."

We chilled for the rest of the day until we had to get ready for the party.

One by one, the guests arrived. Each dressed more glamorously than the previous. I didn't breathe properly until Lex and Emery arrived.

Emery came straight to me and gave me a tight hug.

"Hey, you," he said, sounding choked.

"What's the matter?"

"Nothing. Are you okay?"

I nodded. "Yes."

"And Frederick?"

"He's...okay too, I think."

He gave me a look I couldn't quite understand before he left me to greet Frederick's mom and his parents.

At dinner, we sat next to Emery and Lex. They were so great together. A little pang of jealousy came over me. I'd never had anyone look at me like Lex did Emery. Like he'd die if Emery wasn't there.

There was a very good reason for it. After everything they'd been through to be together, they'd earned their happy ever after. They had a truly special connection.

Occasionally, I glanced at Frederick and wondered what he wanted in a partner. Who would be the person who'd steal his attention away from me? We'd then just be friends who occasionally saw each other.

"Hey," he whispered in my ear. "What's up? You look sad."

"I'm okay. Just having a great time."

He put his arm around my waist and pulled me closer. When his lips landed on my hair, I wanted to cry.

I held on until after dessert was served. When everyone moved to the living area by the Christmas tree for coffee, I saw my opportunity.

I excused myself and, like the night before, ran to the bedroom. Frederick's family was going to think I was a drama queen, but right now, I didn't care. I needed to feel like I could breathe again.

"Ren, are you okay? Did I do something wrong?"

I turned to Frederick, who'd followed me up, closing the bedroom door behind him.

"I'm sorry, Frederick, but I can't do this. I can't be your fake boyfriend."

"Why?"

I ran my hands over my hair. "Because while you're there staking your claim, running your hands all over my back, being the sweetest, most perfect boyfriend in the world, it's killing me inside. I didn't mean for it to happen, but I can't be as unaffected as you are."

"You're affected by me?" he asked, slowly walking toward me as if afraid to make the wrong move.

"Don't play dumb. You know how you look. I haven't been with anyone since Chad, and even then, we didn't have a healthy relationship. You're so amazing." I swallowed the lump in my throat. "My heart wants to get carried away pretending this is real when my head knows it's not. I know it's easy for you because you're straight, but maybe...maybe you can back off a little so I don't get the wrong idea?"

"What if you don't have the wrong idea?"

I walked back until I felt my butt hit the dresser.

"What?"

He let out a long breath and scratched the back of his neck. "I'm not as straight as you think I am, Ren."

"What are you saying?"

"Ren." He closed the gap between us, placing his hands on both my cheeks. I met his intense gaze. The same kind I'd wished for earlier. "It's funny how life works because I lied to my mom to stop her matchmaking and then found myself falling in love with the person I least expected."

I shook my head.

"You burst into my orderly life with your succulents and bright clothes, those shorts that hug your legs and show every delicious curve in your body. You turned me inside out. My whole life, I thought my attraction to men was because I'd been living a lie and my brain had accepted it. After meeting you, I knew I just hadn't met the right man who'd take all those questions away."

"How can you be sure?"

He ran his thumbs over my lips. "Because I've never wanted to kiss anyone, man or woman, as much as I want to kiss you. I've never wanted to take care of and worship someone so much. Ren, you've taken root in my heart. This is forever, baby. At least for me, but if you—"

I stopped his rambling by pressing my mouth against his. When our lips met, the world stopped. Frederick kissed me like he'd wanted to do it for a lifetime and had only just been given permission. I gave myself over to the kiss, squashing all my doubts and fears.

His mouth was warm, wet, and still tasted like chocolate from the dessert. I moaned with every pass of his tongue over mine.

Frederick picked me up and sat me on the dresser, where the increased height put us at a more even level. I wrapped my arms around his shoulders, feeling his muscles rippling underneath as his hands caressed every part of my body.

"Frederick," I moaned between kisses.

"God, I want you so much."

"Want you too."

He reached for the button on my shorts and pried them open. I'd debated wearing something more appropriate for dinner, but Frederick had asked me to be myself because I'd feel more comfortable than trying to fit the image I thought other people wanted to see.

The loose fabric gave him easy access. I cried out when he touched my hard cock over my underwear.

"You have no idea how long I've waited for this, Laurence Oliver. How I never thought it would happen."

"Frederick!" I gasped as he pushed the elastic band of my underwear down to free my cock. He wrapped his hand around my hardness and gave it a few strokes.

"My dreams and fantasies don't even come close to how perfect this is."

"Please," I rasped. "Let me...you too."

He let go of my cock to undo the buttons on his dress pants before pushing his underwear down and placing my hand on his cock.

His mouth crashed into mine again, so I couldn't see it,

but fuck, I could feel it. He was big and uncut. My ass would have a field day with his dick.

We stroked until we orgasmed together, panting, our mouths still fused.

"Oh my god, has this really just happened?" I gasped, still trying to get my breathing back.

"Stay here," Frederick said, pulling his pants up and going to the bathroom. He came back a moment later with a wet cloth. He cleaned me up and helped me out of the shorts. Most of our combined release was pooling in the folds of them.

I found myself naked from the waist down while Frederick was fully dressed.

I reached over to my bag, but he caught me by the waist and took me to the bed.

"We're going to talk now before you freak out."

Frederick

"Freak out? Me?" Ren asked, his voice rising to a high pitch.

I chuckled.

"I want to get dressed," he said.

"Would you be more comfortable if I was undressed too?"

He seemed to think about it. "Okay."

I removed my clothes and his shirt and maneuvered us under the covers.

"You're very tense for someone who just had a mind-blowing orgasm."

"Mind-blowing?"

I raised a brow. "I was there, remember?"

He smiled.

"Can I make a confession?" he asked.

"Of course." He closed his eyes as I played with his hair.

"The first time I saw you wearing that ridiculous outfit

to your date with Emery, I wanted to chuck a jug of water over your head."

I laughed. "This isn't where I thought this was going."

"Shush, it's my turn now. You don't want me to freak out. This is me not freaking out."

"Okay, so you wanted to do terrible things to me that night."

"No," he pointed out. "I wanted to do terrible things to your outfit. That was a crime against fashion, and everyone who had to watch you wear it should have been compensated."

I laughed. "Don't spare my feelings."

"I think I made them clear that night." He cuddled up to me and ran his hand over my chest. "When you turned up at the club the night I was out with Emery and Lex, I felt so vulnerable. I'd failed at my relationship and screwed up my opportunity to have my dream business."

"Ren, that's not true. Chad ruined your relationship, and I'm glad he did because otherwise, we wouldn't be here. I should send him a gift or something."

"You'll do no such thing."

I laughed. "Whatever you want, baby."

"I like it when you call me that. Or sweetheart. I used to hate it. It made me hope that you really meant it."

"I did mean it."

"I know that now."

I put my hand under his chin so I could look into his eyes. "How about all the flirting, teasing, and innuendos?"

"I was testing you and giving myself reminders. I thought the more uncomfortable you were, the more it proved that you were straight and we could never be together."

"I'm sorry I didn't tell you how I felt earlier," I confessed. "I was afraid to ruin our friendship. Any time you mentioned an attractive man, he was always the polar opposite of me. I never thought I stood a chance."

Ren pulled my face closer and kissed me gently. "It was another reminder."

"The only reminders you're allowed now are those that tell you how hard, fast, and deep I've fallen for you, Ren."

"How are you so okay with this?"

I planted small kisses on his cheek, jaw, and neck. My dick stirred against his thigh. "It was a shock at first, I'll admit. I'd been attracted to men before, but with you, it was different. Once I got used to feeling this way, it all clicked into place. I think I may be bisexual, but honestly? I don't care. The only person I want in my life from now on is you."

"Do you remember when I told you I loved you that night I got drunk because of Chad?"

I nodded.

"I was telling the truth. I was so angry with myself because I'd just gotten rid of Chad, a lying bastard closet case, and then I found myself catching feelings for you. I hated myself for that."

"You were afraid you were once again on the wrong side of love."

"Yes."

"There are no wrong sides, Ren. Just us, and we'll always be on the right side of love."

He moved to straddle me. I groaned when my cock became wedged between his ass cheeks.

"Ren, you're killing me."

"I love you so much, Frederick. I'm glad I don't have to pretend anymore."

"Me too. God, I can't get enough of you. Please tell me we can do more before I explode."

"No! We're not having sex in your mother's house while you have a room full of guests downstairs."

I smirked. "And hand jobs aren't sex?"

"I was caught unprepared. You were very...persuasive."

I ran my hand over his stomach, smiling when my hand touched his already hard cock.

"Your body is telling me you want another orgasm."

He huffed. "My body is stupid."

"Oh, I don't know. It seems to know who it wants. I'd say your body is pretty smart."

"And you're pretty cocky."

"Only for you, baby."

I flipped us over so I was on top of him. Our cocks rubbed together, making us both catch our breath.

"People," he gasped. "Downstairs."

"It's only us up here."

"Lex and Emery will know what we're up to."

"How much do you want to bet they've already left?" I moved down his body, caressing and kissing every inch of his milky-white skin.

The patch of blond hair that had teased me the other week was now a free runway down to the most perfect cock.

Not that I had much to compare it to, but Ren's was perfect.

My mouth watered, wanting to taste him. Should I be a little more apprehensive or reluctant? Maybe, but I think I'd been in the process of discovering and accepting my bisexuality even before I met Ren. He was simply the catalyst that threw me over the edge.

My lips closed around his cockhead, and he moaned, raising his hips. What I felt for causing him to be like this was humbling but empowering.

As my confidence grew, I took more of him into my mouth.

"Fuck yes, that feels so good," he moaned.

I wanted to make him spill in my mouth. Taste him. But at the same time, I wanted to bury myself in him. Look into his eyes as he came with me.

"Ren, I need to be inside you."

He sighed. "Please."

I reached over to the nightstand, which was when I remembered we weren't at the apartment. There were no condoms or lube.

"Shit."

"What's up?"

"I don't have anything here."

"I have a packet of lube in my bag but no condoms."

I jumped out of bed to grab his bag. The lube was easy to find, but there were no condoms. "I've been on PrEP for a week, and I tested negative prior," I said.

"Wait, you're on PrEP?"

I nodded. "I had a conversation with Emery. He told

me to pay attention to you. I think he wanted me to notice you noticing me. That gave me the courage to consider coming out to you. I saw my doctor the next day."

"I'm negative. I tested after Chad cheated on me, and I've been on PrEP for years."

I huffed a laugh. "We're doing this."

"We are. I now have a very inconvenient erection, so despite my better judgment, I declare you have to deal with it."

I grabbed the packet of lube and slathered my cock, dropping what I hoped was enough on my fingers.

"Let me know if I hurt you, okay? I've never done this before."

"Okay."

My fingers trembled as I reached down to the puckered pink flesh. A million ideas passed through my mind. Licking it, sucking it, fucking it with my tongue. All those things made my dick even harder.

How could I have ever thought I wasn't attracted to men? It seemed like such a ridiculous idea now.

Ren's little sounds of pleasure were the most powerful aphrodisiac. I pushed a finger through the ring of muscles. It was so much tighter than I'd imagined.

"Fuck, how will I ever fit in there? You're so tight."

"You'll fit. Trust me. Your big cock was made for my ass. I guarantee it."

I trusted him. I just didn't trust I wouldn't lose my mind when I felt that hot pressure surrounding my cock.

Ren encouraged me to add more fingers until he said he was relaxed and open enough to take me.

At least one of us was relaxed.

"I need you now. Please, Frederick."

I added more lube to my length and pressed it against Ren's hole. There was resistance at first, but as he relaxed further, I felt like I was being sucked into a hole of blissful pleasure.

"God, you're tight."

"And you're fucking huge."

I gritted through my teeth. "I'd take it as a compliment, but right now, I'm trying not to come and especially not to hurt you."

I inched a little forward.

"Hurt me, Frederick. Fucking ruin me for anyone else."

I groaned and pushed the rest of the way until my balls rested against his ass.

"Fuck, fuck," I moaned.

Ren took my face in his hands. "I'm almost there, okay? Just a few seconds to adjust, and then you can move. I promise you won't hurt me."

I nodded.

Those seconds felt like years. Sweat beaded down my forehead, landing on Ren's.

He moved under me, giving me the sign.

I pulled back a little and then pushed forward a few times until Ren was moaning all kinds of incoherent words.

The pressure on my dick was too much. I could already feel the tell-tale signs of an impending orgasm.

"Do I need to jack you off?" I asked.

He shook his head. "Just keep the pace." He raised one of his legs over my shoulder. "Like that. Harder."

I gave him everything I had and more.

"Oh god, yes. That feels so good. You're hitting the right spot. Of fuck, I'm—" That was all he said before he came all over his belly without even needing to use his hands.

I was mesmerized, staring at the sight in front of me. The cum pooling in the dip of his belly, his blissful post-orgasmic expression.

My orgasm tore through me like a bullet, and even though I'd come at his hand only an hour ago, I still felt like it was the most intense orgasm I'd ever had.

"How was that possible?" I asked, still catching my breath.

"What?"

"You came without touching yourself."

He laughed. "I forgot this was your first time."

"Technically second, but details..."

"Well, my gorgeous, well-endowed, beautiful, kind...man—"

"Boyfriend," I interrupted.

He smiled wide. "Boyfriend...what happened was that my ass loved the size of your dick and especially the way you kept rubbing my prostate. I used to think it was a myth, but your dick has proved me wrong."

"I guess we can continue to test this theory for a long, long time."

He yawned. "I'm very okay with that."

"Come on, let's grab a shower before we're perma-nently stuck together."

Another yawn. "What's the problem?"

I had zero problems being stuck to Ren for the rest of my life. Something I whispered over and over again as we showered together.

As we settled in bed, Ren falling asleep in the same position he'd woken up in this morning, I wondered two things: how early could we leave here tomorrow and was this truly my new reality.

Ren

Christmas Day

A loud bark woke me up. I pulled a pillow over my head, but it was pulled back.

"Go away," I demanded.

Another bark.

"You know he won't stop until you give him some attention."

I turned around and was immediately greeted by Melon's wet tongue all over my face.

"Ew, this isn't how I wanted to be woken up on Christmas Day."

Frederick sat on the side of the bed by my hip and leaned forward for a kiss.

"Merry Christmas, baby."

I harumphed. "Why am I not waking up with your dick inside me?"

He laughed. "Because my balls need a rest, and you need to sit through dinner with your family."

I smiled. I couldn't wait to tell my parents and Winnie about Frederick and me. I knew they already liked him, so I hoped they'd be happy for us.

Frederick's parents had called us last night from Paris. They had a Christmas Day cruise booked, so they'd wished us an early Merry Christmas.

"So what do we do until it's time to head out?" I asked.

"I was thinking we could start with breakfast, then take Melon for a walk so he behaves in the car, and if you've been a really, *really* good boy, I might give you a blowjob."

I grabbed his shirt and pulled him closer. "I've been a really good boy. I even wrote a letter to Santa."

"Oh really? Then maybe this is why this thing has appeared on my desk."

"What thing?"

He gestured for Melon to jump up on the bed again, and I noticed he had a red bow around his neck.

"I already know Melon is my present. I don't need to unwrap it."

"That's not what I'm talking about," he said.

I searched for a clue, avoiding Melon's eager display of affection until I found a small piece of paper attached to the ribbon. I pulled it off and unrolled it.

"It's a QR code."

I looked at Frederick, and he passed me my phone.

I scanned the code, and it took me to a website.

"What's this?" I zoomed in on the flower shop storefront that was advertised on the website.

"You don't have to take this route, but I wanted to offer you the option. Years ago, Mr. Livingston invested in a business. That's what he did and what I now do for him. This particular business, a flower store, has been in the hands of the same couple for over thirty years. They want to retire but have no one to leave the business to since they have no children. Mr. Livingston told me to sell it, but I think it should remain an investment...for you."

"What?" I looked at him and then back at the phone. "The store could be mine? But how could I afford it? I haven't saved enough money."

He took my hands in his. "Please listen all the way to the end, okay? I don't want to take away your independence, and I think what you're doing is amazing. So many people would have given up by now. I also know a good investment when I see it. I'm not planning on letting you go ever, so your success as a business owner is also in my best interests. I have a trust fund I've never used and will sit there gathering dust and earning a pittance in interest. If you'd like to have me as your silent partner, I'd love to invest in the store with you. You can use the money you've saved for all the improvements to buy stock and to get all set up to trade."

My hands shook in his. He raised them to his mouth and kissed each knuckle.

"Is this real?"

"It's as real as you want it to be, Ren. I can put the business on the market and sell it to someone who might not care enough about flowers and making people happy. Or I can be with you as you walk through the door of your new dream."

Tears fell down my face. The highlight of the last week was Frederick and I officially becoming a couple, but I was exhausted.

Juggling so many jobs was becoming too much. Even now that I was sleeping in a nice bed and in Frederick's arms every night, I'd upped my hours wherever I could, which meant I was often a walking zombie.

Would it be so hard to take this offer? Would it make my achievement any less if I had the support of a business partner? Or would accepting it mean I was a good businessman who knew an opportunity when it came?

"Yes. I'd love that very much." As soon as I said it, I knew it was the right decision. "We'll have to work through the terms, and I need more details, but I'm tired of doing jobs I'm not passionate about and feeling like the one thing I'm meant to do is always one step too far."

Frederick hugged me tight. "I can't wait to see you become the businessman I know you'll be. Everyone in the city will flock to your store. Just watch."

I certainly hoped so.

"So, how about that blowjob?" I asked, taking one of his hands and placing it on my erection.

"Ren, you're the worst."

I shrugged. "Not my fault you're a fast learner and I can't get enough of you."

"A charmer, as always."

He pulled me off the bed and took me in a fireman's lift into the kitchen.

"I'm naked!"

His eyes roamed my body from head to toe as he put me down on the kitchen table.

"So you are. Open up." He pointed to my mouth and gave me a piece of strawberry. Bit by bit, he fed me a breakfast of pancakes, fruit, and chocolate sauce.

The sauce somehow mostly ended up on my dick, so I hoped he had the intention of cleaning me up. After all, this was his mess.

Melon's walk ended up being a little later than planned and cut in half. We also arrived at my parents' twenty minutes late, which earned us a scolding from Winnie, who only forgave us when we said Frederick was now my boyfriend.

My parents couldn't have been happier, and we talked about them meeting Frederick's parents sometime soon.

My heart filled with joy as I looked around the table at all the people I loved.

I'd lived on scraps for the longest time, thinking they were all I was worth. Sometimes, it took someone else showing us our value to truly believe it.

I'd so easily recognized my sister's musical talent that I'd given up my inheritance to ensure she could fulfill her potential. It was a decision I hadn't regretted so far, even if she decided she didn't want to go to Juilliard.

It was becoming easier to make decisions when I knew I had the support of the man I loved.

I took his hand and asked him to follow me to my old room upstairs.

"What's up? We're not having sex in your parents' house," he said.

I raised a brow. "Double standards, Mr. Rhys-Myr."

He nodded and pointed at the door missing a lock, not to mention that my parents' house was much smaller than his parents' and would make any sexual activity impossible.

"I just wanted to say that by this time next year, I want us to be walking down the aisle. I don't need a ring or an expensive ceremony. I just need you, Frederick. I've made many stupid decisions in my life, but letting you hold my hand and protect me was the smartest one of all."

"Oh, Ren. I love you so much," he said before he covered my lips with his.

I opened the drawer on the nightstand and pulled out something I'd made years ago.

"What's that?"

"It's a daisy chain. It represents our friendship, our connection, and our love. It will go around and around. Maybe some daisies will fall off and others will be added. We'll need to check for the stability of the foundations, but I know we both care enough about it to make it last forever."

"Dammit, Ren. I will fucking marry you right now."

I laughed. "Patience. I don't want anything extravagant, but I still need to shop for an outfit."

He claimed my lips again, and we made out until we were interrupted by a nosy little sister and a hungry puppy.

Best Christmas Ever.

I hope you enjoyed Frederick and Ren's story. The Christmas Roommate is also available as an audiobook on Audible, narrated by Alexander Cendese.

Ren and Frederick first appeared in The Lost Fiancé Twist. If you're curious to find out how Emery and Lex got their story, you can read it now.

The Lost Fiancé Twist is also available on Amazon and on Audible, narrated by Alexander Cendese, and you can pre-order The Fake Husband Deal now.

Read The Lost Fiancé Twist here.

Preorder The Fake Husband Deal here.

Sign up for my newsletter to get all the latest news.

Sign up here.

Books by Ana Ashley

Single Dads of Stillwater

A spin off series from Chester Falls that can be read on its own. Each book features one or more single dads in this community of friends, family and found family. In this contemporary MM romance series you'll find heat, emotion and a guaranteed happy ever after.

Newcomer

Antagonist

Breakthrough

Heartstring

Datebook (Coming soon)

Finding You Series

A standalone series set across the Atlantic between New York and Portugal. Find your way home with this contemporary MM romance series with friends to lovers, star-crossed lovers and age gap with plenty of heat, feels and always a happy ever after.

Home Again

Together Again

Love Again

And for a special short story, Complete Again, plus bonus scenes, grab the Finding You boxset now.

Room for 3 series

This is a high heat MMM contemporary romance series set in an island resort.

The Resort

The Vacation

Chester Falls Series

From a Prince to a Happy Ever After for all, enjoy this small town MM romance series that's as sweet as they come, with plenty of heat, humor and everything in between.

How to Catch a Bookworm (Prequel short)

How to Catch a Prince

How to Catch a Rival

How to Catch a Bodyguard

How to Catch a Bachelor

How to Catch the Boss (a Christmas novella)

How to Catch a Biker

How to Catch a Vet

How to Catch a Happy Ever After

Standalone books

Christmas Bubble: a low angst, standalone, Christmas novel featuring a petite but larger-than-life cheerleader, an older demisexual football coach and a winter cabin by the lake with only one bed. With cameos from Chester Falls and Stillwater.

Midnight Ash: a sweet Cinderella fairytale retelling with a sexy kinky twist on the side, and a cast who don't quite behave as you'd expect.

Stronghold: a sweet and sexy romance in Sarina Bowen's World of True North, Vino & Veritas series. This is a standalone story between two childhood friends who reunite after as decade apart, with some creative use of maple syrup.

FREE READS

My Fake Billionaire - Amazon (readerlinks.com/l/1666958)

My Fake Billionaire - All stores (https://books2read.com/u/3n8zW6)

The Vacation - BookHip.com/NBQNQKR

Ana Ashley was born in Portugal but has lived in the United Kingdom for so long, even her friends sometimes doubt if she really is Portuguese.

After getting hooked on reading gay romance, Ana decided to follow her lifelong dream of becoming an author.

These days you can find her in front of her laptop bringing her stories to life, or in the kitchen perfecting her recipe for the famous Portuguese custard tarts.

Ana Ashley writes sweet and steamy gay romance set in America, often in small towns where everyone knows everyone.

You can follow Ana on the usual social media hangouts.

For access to exclusive teasers, content, and general book and food related goodness you can now join Ana in her Facebook Group, Café RoMMance - Ana's Reader Group (facebook.com/groups/208814836439843/)

Ana's VIP Readers - bit.ly/AnaAshley

Facebook Page - @anawritesmm

Email - ana@anaashley.com
Instagram - @anawritesmm
Bookbub - bookbub.com/authors/ana-ashley
Goodreads - goodreads.com/ana-ashley